Elliot

Julie Pearson

Manon Gauthier

Translated by Erin Woods

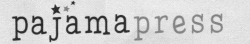

First published in the United States and Canada in 2016
Text copyright © 2016 Julie Pearson
Illustration copyright © 2016 Manon Gauthier
This edition copyright © 2016 Pajama Press Inc.
Translated from French by Erin Woods
Originally published in French by éditions Les 400 coups.

10 9 8 7 6 5 4 3 2 1

www.pajamapress.ca   info@pajamapress.ca

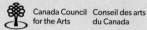

The publisher gratefully acknowledges the support of the Canada Council for the Arts and the
Ontario Arts Council for its publishing program. We acknowledge the financial support of the
Government of Canada through the Canada Book Fund (CBF) for our publishing activities.

Library and Archives Canada Cataloguing in Publication
Pearson, Julie, 1978-
[Elliot. English]
      Elliot / Julie Pearson ; [illustrated by] Manon Gauthier.
Translation of: Elliot.
ISBN 978-1-927485-85-9 (bound)
      I. Gauthier, Manon, 1959-, illustrator II. Title. III. Title: Elliot. English
PS8631.E325E4413 2015   jC843'.6   C2015-902334-3

Publisher Cataloging-in-Publication Data (U.S.)
Pearson, Julie, 1978 -
    Elliot / Julie Pearson ; illustrated by Manon Gauthier.
Originally published in French by les Éditions Les 400 coups, 2014.
[32] pages : color illustrations ; cm.
Summary: "Elliot's parents do not know how to take care of him. As Elliot moves from one foster
home to another, his visits with his real parents leave him anxious and conflicted about where he
wants to be. At last he finds stability with a new adoptive family" – Provided by publisher.
ISBN-13: 978-1-92748-585-9
1. Orphans – Juvenile fiction. 2. Foster parents – Juvenile fiction. 3. Rabbits – Juvenile fiction.
I. Gauthier, Manon. II. Title.
[E] dc23   PZ7.1.P437EI 2015

Manufactured by Sheck Wah Tong Printing Ltd.
Printed in Hong Kong, China

Pajama Press Inc.
181 Carlaw Ave. Suite 207 Toronto, Ontario Canada, M4M 2S1

Distributed in Canada by UTP Distribution
5201 Dufferin Street Toronto, Ontario Canada, M3H 5T8

Distributed in the U.S. by Ingram Publisher Services
1 Ingram Blvd. La Vergne, TN 37086, USA

To my Coco.
—J.P.

To Nellie, Mary Ann, Alice,
and Stanley
—M.G.

This is the story of Elliot, a playful little boy who was full of life.
His mother and father loved him very much.

BUT...
When Elliot cried, his mother and his father did not understand why.

When Elliot yelled,
his mother and his father did not know what to do.

When Elliot misbehaved,
his mother and his father did not know how to react.

One day, Elliot's parents asked for help. That's when Thomas came to visit.

He said he would take Elliot to stay with another family until his parents learned how to take better care of him.

So Thomas took Elliot to a new family, where there was a new mother and a new father to welcome him.

Elliot did not understand what was happening. It worried him so much that he wanted to cry.

In this new family, everything was different.

The smells were different. The toys were different. And there was a big cat that followed him everywhere.

BUT IN THIS FAMILY...

When Elliot cried, they understood he was hungry.

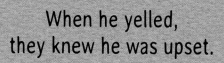

When he yelled,
they knew he was upset.

When he misbehaved, they realized he needed attention.

Often, Elliot's mother and father came to play with him.

One day, Thomas told Elliot that he could go home
with his mother and father.

They were ready to take care of him again.
They were so excited to bring him home.

Elliot did want to go with his parents.
But it worried him so much that he wanted to yell.

A few months passed. When Thomas visited
the family, he saw that...

When Elliot cried,
his mother and his father did not always understand why.

AAAAAAA

When Elliot yelled,
his mother and his father did not always know what to do.

When Elliot misbehaved,
his mother and his father did not always know how to react.

So Thomas took Elliot to a new family,
where there was a new mother and a new father
and three new children to welcome him.

In this new family, everything was different.

The smells were different. The toys were different. And there was
a big bird that sang too loudly.

BUT IN THIS FAMILY...

When Elliot cried, they understood he was hungry.

When he yelled, they knew he was upset.

When he misbehaved, they realized he needed attention.

Often, Elliot's mother and father came to play with him.

Even though Elliot was happy with his new family,
he still wanted to go home with his mother and father. And it worried him
so much that he wanted to misbehave.

One day, Thomas came to visit Elliot.
He explained that Elliot's parents could never take care of him,
because they did not know how.

Thomas said he would look for a new family for Elliot—
a forever, forever family.

Elliot understood that this was important news. And it worried him
so much that he wanted to cry, yell, and misbehave.

Eventually, Thomas found a new family where there was a new mother and a new father and a new big brother to welcome him. Elliot did not understand everything, but he could tell that they were happy to have him.

In this new family, everything was different.
The smells were different. The toys were different.
And there was a big dog that sniffed everything.

BUT MOST OF ALL, IN THIS FAMILY...
When Elliot cried, they dried his tears.

When he yelled, they listened to him.

When he misbehaved, they loved him anyway.

In time, Elliot grew attached to his new family.

When he cried or yelled or misbehaved, his new parents would hold him in their arms and tell him they loved him forever, forever.

Sometimes, Elliot's mother and father still came to play with him. Every time they did, he was afraid it would be the end of his new life—and it worried him so much that he wanted to run away.

His new parents reminded him:
"You are a part of our family now—forever, FOREVER."

One day, Thomas came to visit Elliot and his new family.
Elliot was afraid he would have to leave again.
Then, Thomas announced that he was officially adopted.

He would never have to change families again.

THERE WAS A PARTY.

And since that day, every night,
Elliot treasures the words his new parents whisper in his ear:

"I love you forever, FOREVER..."